Dora the Explorer in . . .

WoRLd SchooL Day AdVenTuRe

Based on the TV series *Dora the Explorer*™ as seen on NickJr.™

SIMON SPOTLIGHT/NICKELODEON
An imprint of Simon & Schuster Children's Publishing Division
1230 Avenue of the Americas, New York, New York 10020
© 2010 Viacom International Inc. All rights reserved. NICKELODEON,
NICK JR., *Dora the Explorer,* and all related titles,
logos, and characters are trademarks of Viacom International Inc.
All rights reserved, including the right of reproduction in whole or in part in any form.
SIMON SPOTLIGHT and colophon are registered trademarks of Simon & Schuster, Inc.
For information about special discounts for bulk purchases, please contact Simon & Schuster
Special Sales at 1-866-506-1949 or business@simonandschuster.com.
Design by James Salerno
Manufactured in the United States of America 0910 LAK
First Edition
2 4 6 8 10 9 7 5 3 1
ISBN 978-1-4424-1673-4

With special thanks to (in alphabetical order):
Paula Allen • Jon Anderson • Leigh Anne Brodsky • Brian Bromberg • Jose Carbonell • Giuseppe Castellano • Siobhan Ciminera
Doug Cohn • Rosemary Contreras • Roger Estrada • Cathy Galeota • Valerie Garfield • Chris Gifford • Russell Hicks
Ceci Kurzman • Jaime Levine • Mercedes McDonald • Rhonda Medina • Raina Moore • Kellee Riley • James Salerno
Patricia Short • Russell Spina • Kuni Tomita • Valerie Walsh Valdes • Teri Weiss • Cyma Zargharni

Dora the Explorer in . . .

WoRLd ScHooL Day AdvenTure

written by Shakira

illustrated by
Kuni Tomita & Kellee Riley

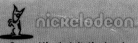

Simon Spotlight/Nickelodeon
New York   London   Toronto   Sydney

It was World School Day, and Dora and Boots were super excited. Today they would be a part of a big celebration with kids from schools all over the world.

"Kids everywhere are going to connect online using laptops," Dora explained to Boots. "It'll be a big *fiesta! ¡Vamos!*" And with that, they raced into the school.

Inside the Rainforest School, everyone was busy getting ready for the big day. There were balloons and banners and a very special guest: Shakira!

"I love World School Day," said Shakira. "It's the day when students from all around the world make sure they have everything they need for a great school year! We'll see new schools, meet new friends, and with these new laptops, kids can log on to the World School Day *fiesta* and we'll sing a very special song together!"

Just then, Shakira's cell phone rang. She spoke quietly, but as her face turned from happy to concerned, Dora and Boots knew something was wrong. "The school in Ethiopia is missing its laptops," Shakira told them as she hung up. "If the students don't have laptops, they won't be able to join the World School Day *fiesta*."

Dora knew that something needed to be done, and fast. "We can help!" she said. "Maybe we can find a way to share some of our laptops with the school in Ethiopia."

"*Gracias, Dora*," said Shakira.

"*La Maestra* Beatriz," said Dora, running up to her teacher. "The school in Ethiopia doesn't have any laptops. Can we share some of ours with them?"

"Of course," *La Maestra* Beatriz replied.
"Sharing is a great idea!"

"*Gracias*," said Dora. "Let's go!"

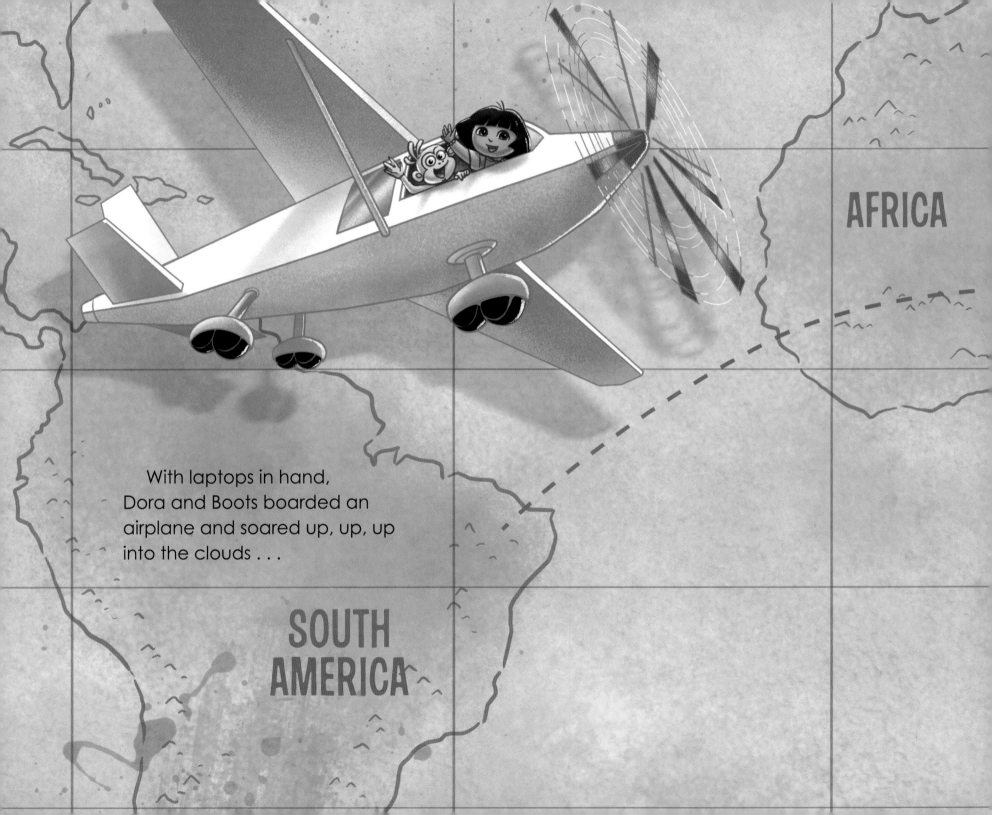

AFRICA

With laptops in hand,
Dora and Boots boarded an
airplane and soared up, up, up
into the clouds . . .

SOUTH
AMERICA

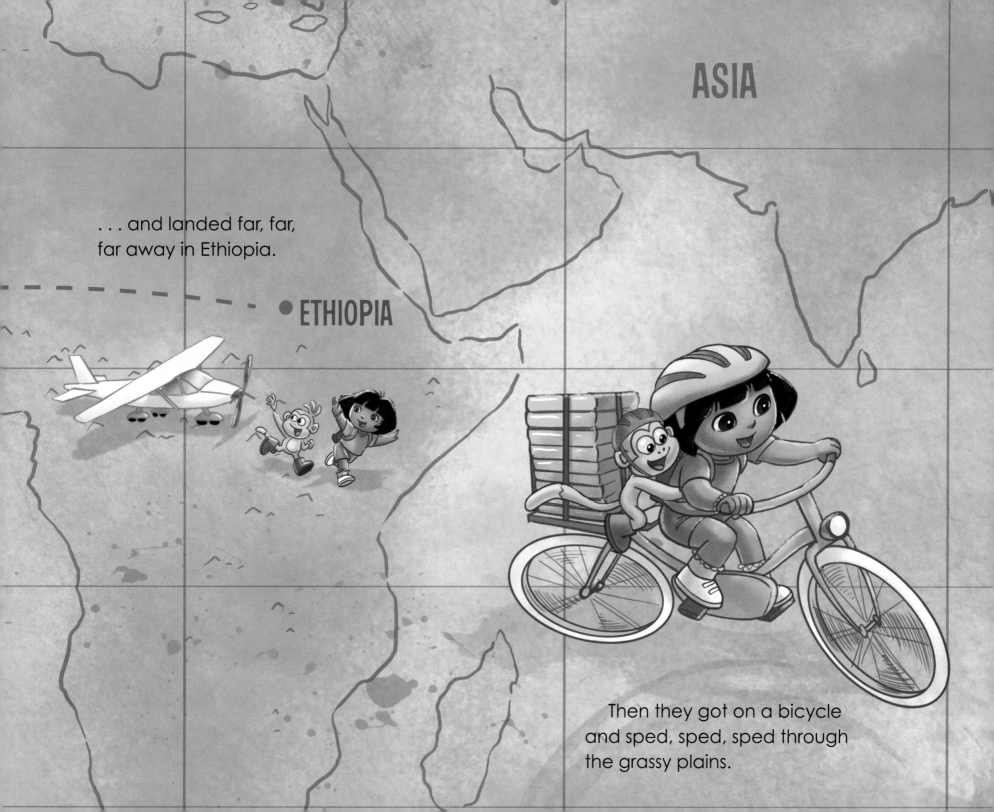

ASIA

. . . and landed far, far,
far away in Ethiopia.

●ETHIOPIA

Then they got on a bicycle
and sped, sped, sped through
the grassy plains.

Dora and Boots looked left, right, and all around, but didn't see any schools. In the distance, they heard some happy whispers and giggles.

"I think someone's reading a story," said Boots.

"And it's coming from under that tree," agreed Dora.

As they moved closer, Dora and Boots saw a big, beautiful tree that sat in the middle of a school.

A girl waved to them. "I'm Makeda," she said. "Welcome to the School-Under-a-Tree!"

"Wow, a school under a tree!" Boots did a backflip. "That's so awesome!"

"Kids and teachers have been gathering under this tree for classes even before the school was built," Makeda explained. "Are those laptops?"

"Yeah!" exclaimed Dora. "The students of the Rainforest School wanted to share them with your school. Now we can all join the World School Day *fiesta*!"

"Hooray!" said the students.

Dora set up her laptop and was showing the kids where she and Boots went to school when it started to beep. It was Shakira.

"The school in India is ready for the *fiesta*, but is missing supplies. The students need twelve school kits filled with crayons, pencils, notebooks, and glue," said Shakira. "Without those kits, they won't be ready for the school year. Can you help?"

"*Sí podemos!*" said Dora, even though she wasn't sure where she would get the kits. Makeda whispered something in her teacher's ear. As soon as the teacher nodded yes, Makeda smiled. "Yay! We can share our school kits with the kids in India!"

"*Gracias,* Makeda," said Dora. "Come on, Boots. Let's go!"

With school kits in hand, Dora and Boots boarded a train that chugged, chugged, chugged down the tracks . . .

AFRICA

ETHIOPIA

ASIA

. . . until they arrived far,
far, far away in India.

● INDIA

Then they got on a
moped and zoomed,
zoomed, zoomed
through the city.

Dora and Boots searched high and low. They didn't see the school, but they heard a loud *Beep! Beep!*

"That sounds like a bus!" said Boots.

Just then a huge bus roared down the street and a group of kids started running toward it.

"I think we found the school!" said Dora.

A woman opened the bus doors and greeted them. "Welcome to the School-on-Wheels. I'm Teacher Ravina!"

"I've never been in a bus that looks like this," said Boots, climbing aboard. "This is a really cool school!"

"The school is a bus so it can go from town to town. That way, more kids can go to school!" said Teacher Ravina.

It was snack time and the teacher offered Dora and Boots some yummy coconut bread.

"¡Delicioso!" said Dora. "And we have something for you too—school kits!"

Teacher Ravina was so happy to have the kits. Now the School-on-Wheels was ready for the school year.

Dora set up her laptop and showed the kids where the school kits came from. "The students from the School-Under-a-Tree in Ethiopia wanted to share them with you," she told them.

Suddenly, Dora's computer beeped. It was Shakira!

"Dora, now a school in Cambodia needs our help. They need twelve math books," Shakira explained.

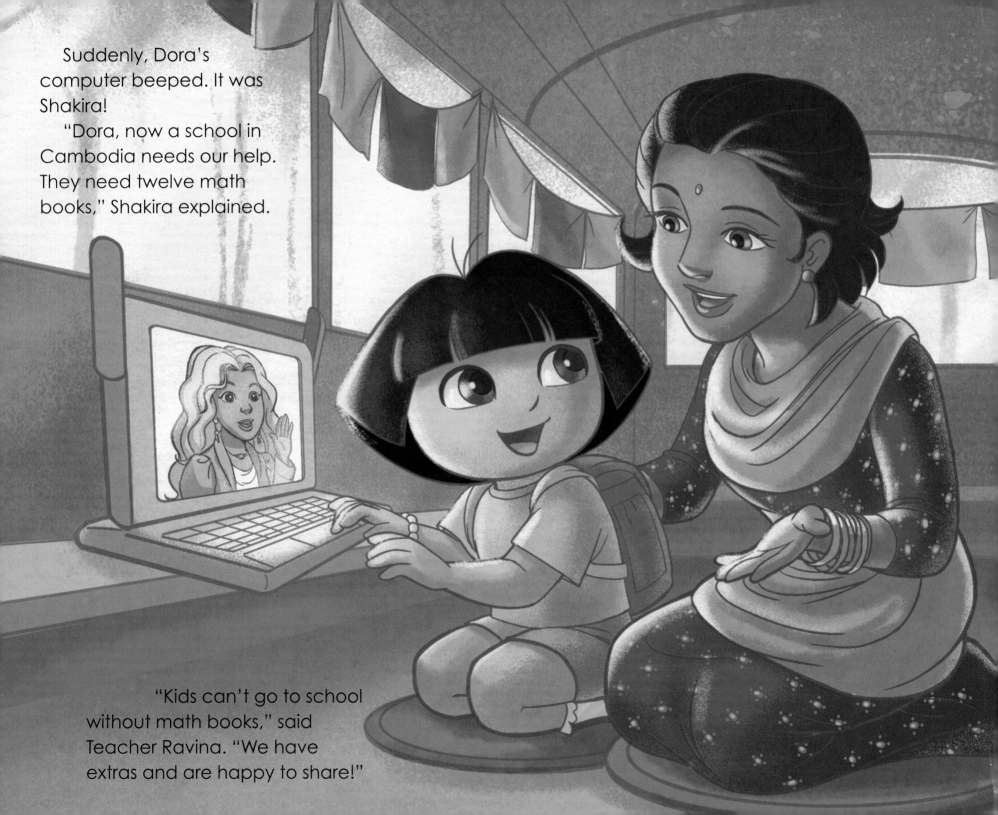

"Kids can't go to school without math books," said Teacher Ravina. "We have extras and are happy to share!"

"¡*Fantástico!*" said Dora.
"Let's go!"

With math books in hand, Dora and Boots climbed atop an elephant who stomped, stomped, stomped across the forest . . .

• INDIA

ASIA

Then they got in a
canoe and paddled
down, down, down,
the winding river.

. . . and arrived far, far,
far away in Cambodia.

● CAMBODIA

As they floated down the river, Dora and
Boots looked all around. They couldn't see
a school anywhere! But they could hear the
sound of soft singing in the distance.

"Could that singing be coming from the school?"
Dora wondered aloud.

The singing grew louder until Dora and Boots were
staring at a school floating on the water! From the deck
and windows, kids sang and waved to them.

With a warm smile, a boy said, "Welcome to the Floating School. I'm Sovann."

"I've never heard of a school that floats," said Boots, jumping up and down with excitement.

"Our school floats so we can roll with the waves if the water gets too rough," Sovann explained.

"Wow, that's really smart," said Dora.

"Here are the books that the students from the School-on-Wheels in India wanted to share with your school," said Dora.

She set up her laptop and showed the kids where the books came from.

All of the kids were excited. Now they would be ready for the school year.

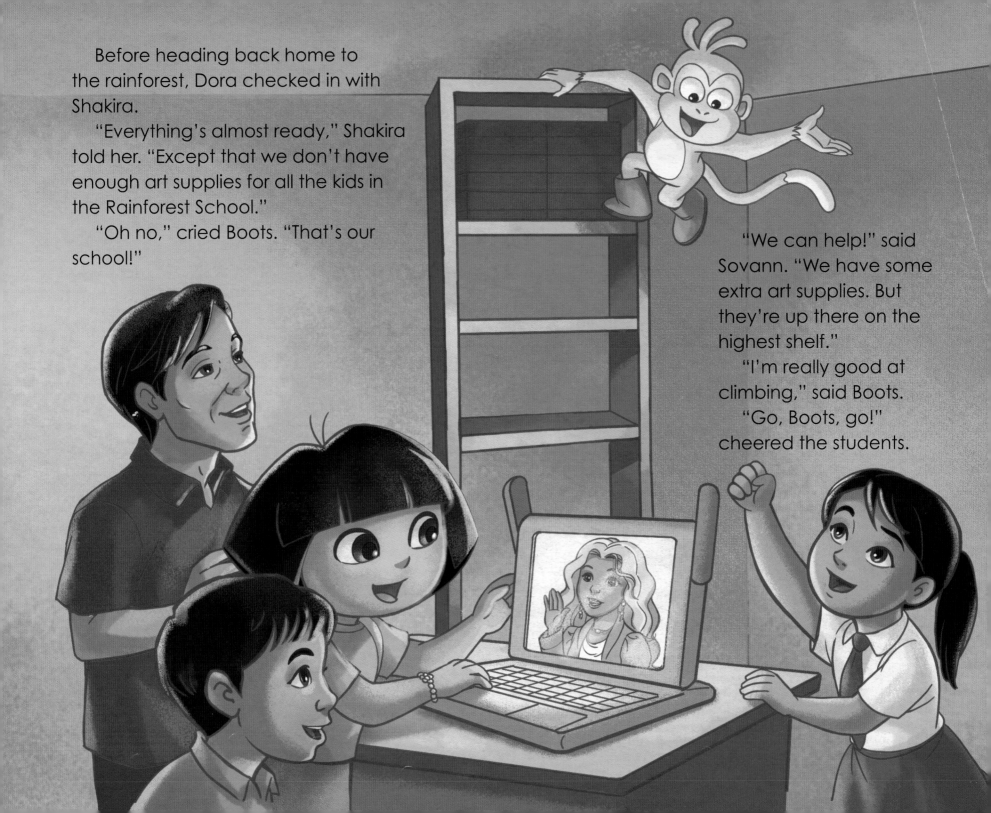

Before heading back home to the rainforest, Dora checked in with Shakira.

"Everything's almost ready," Shakira told her. "Except that we don't have enough art supplies for all the kids in the Rainforest School."

"Oh no," cried Boots. "That's our school!"

"We can help!" said Sovann. "We have some extra art supplies. But they're up there on the highest shelf."

"I'm really good at climbing," said Boots.

"Go, Boots, go!" cheered the students.

With art supplies in hand, Dora and Boots hopped on a hot-air balloon that floated up, up, up into the sky . . .

. . . and landed far, far, far away in the rainforest, where Shakira was waiting for them!

"Were you able to get the art supplies, Dora?" asked Shakira. "We sure did! Now all of the schools are ready!"

Thanks to Dora, Boots, and all of their new friends, everyone was able to share pictures, stories, music, and dances from their World School Day parties. And most important of all—everyone was ready for a great school year!

Shakira picked up her guitar. It was time for the most special part of the day—everyone singing a song—together!

How can you show the world that you care?
Share! Share! Share!
El árbol shares its branches with el ave.
El mar shares its waves with el pez.
El sol shares the sky with la luna.
Tu y yo together can share with others
everything we learn.
How can you show the world that you care?
Share! Share! Share!

"We did it!" shouted Dora.
"*¡Lo hicimos!*" added Shakira. "Together,
friends can always make a difference."

¡Hola, amigos!

I'm so excited to share this book with you. Like Dora, I've always loved exploring, and one of the best ways I know to explore is by reading. Books can take you anywhere—from my hometown in Barranquilla, Colombia, to the North Pole, to lands that only exist in your imagination. Books open up new worlds, no matter where you live.

Kids just like you learn in all kinds of schools, in all sorts of places—in tents, in skyscrapers, on sidewalks, at home, or even through the radio! There are floating schools in places like Cambodia and Vietnam, schools in buses in India, and classes that meet under trees in Ethiopia. But no matter what a classroom looks like, what's important is what schools can do. Learning is what helps you uncover your talents and make your dreams come true.

Unfortunately, not every kid is lucky enough to go to school, but we're helping to change that with this book. This book is helping build schools and support education for children everywhere. So keep reading, keep exploring, and keep dreaming.

Love,
Shakira

A note about the Barefoot Foundation:

The Barefoot Foundation is a United States nonprofit, nongovernmental organization created by internationally acclaimed recording artist and humanitarian Shakira. The Barefoot Foundation is dedicated to ensuring that every child can exercise his or her basic right to a quality education. To date, the Barefoot Foundation and its Colombian partner *Fundación Pies Descalzos* have opened six schools that provide free high-quality education, meals, income-generating projects, and counseling for more then six thousand children and their families. The foundation is currently building its newest school in Haiti. *Pies Descalzos*—or Barefoot—has a double meaning: It is the name of the record that made Shakira's music internationally known, and it represents the thousands of children living in such poverty that they cannot even afford shoes. To learn more and meet some of the foundation's students, visit **barefootfoundation.com**.